3 . . . 2 . . . .

Just then Cassie heard a whirring sound, and slowly, two of the spaceship's panels began to separate. She grabbed the microphone and leapt back. Her eyes darted to the trees. She wanted to make the dash to safety, but suddenly her legs were locked. From between the open panels a small staircase emerged and lowered to the ground. Cassie looked to the top and found herself staring—at a hairless, completely green boy.

Look for the next exciting book in the series
The Spy from Outer Space:

Too Many Spies

Available now!

ALIEN ALERT!

Debra Hess

Illustrated by Carol Newsom

Hyperion Paperbacks for Children
New York

Produced by Chardiet Unlimited, Inc., 33 West 17th Street,
New York, New York 10011.
A Hyperion Paperback original
First edition: September 1993

1   3   5   7   9   10   8   6   4   2

Library of Congress Cataloging-in-Publication Data

Hess, Debra
Alien alert!/Debra Hess—1st ed.
p.   cm.—(The spy from outer space)
Summary: Seeing a spaceship land near her house and meeting one of
its occupants, an alien boy her own age, ten-year-old super spy
Cassie Williams helps him disguise himself as an Earthling and look
for his missing robot.
ISBN 1-56282-567-4
[1. Extraterrestrial beings—Fiction.   2. Science fiction.]
I. Title.   II. Series: Hess, Debra.   Spy from outer space.
PZ7.H4326Al   1993
[FIC]—dc20   95-528
CIP
AC

ALIEN ALERT!

CHAPTER 1

Super Sleuth Cassie Williams lurked outside Hillsdale Elementary School searching for a place to hide. By the time the first group of children arrived, she was crouched behind a clump of bushes. Her new sneakers sunk into the muddy ground, and her spy belt banged against her knees as she peered through binoculars at the approaching students.

Suddenly Cassie's view was blocked. All she could see was pink—hot pink.

"Cassie Williams, what are you doing?"

Cassie lowered the binoculars and looked up. Above the hot-pink skirt and paisley leggings, Marilee Tischler's prissy face frowned down at her.

"Shhh, not so loud," whispered Cassie. "Can't you see I'm on a mission?"

"What kind of a mission?" asked Marilee, even more loudly.

"A spy mission, of course," said Cassie.

"You're going to get all dirty in those bushes."

Cassie couldn't help rolling her eyes. "Oh yeah, Marilee? So what?"

"Sooo . . ." Marilee drew the word out scornfully and placed a hand on her fluorescent hip. "We're in fifth grade now."

"I repeat," said Cassie. "So what?"

"So—we're the oldest class in school," said Marilee. "We have to set an example."

"For whom?"

"Honestly, Cassie." Marilee looked disgusted. "You've been wearing those old jeans and spying on people for as long as I've known you. Aren't you ever going to grow up?"

With a flip of her hair and a flounce of her skirt, Marilee Tischler was gone. Cassie looked after her and sighed. It was the first day of fifth grade, and Marilee was already a problem.

Cassie tried to remember a time when Marilee had *not* been a problem. With her designer clothes and snotty attitude, Marilee was definitely the most "grown-up" girl at Hillsdale Elementary. Worst of all, toward the end of last year, Marilee had discovered flirting. While the rest of the girls in the class were still climbing trees and hating boys, Marilee Tischler was teaching herself how to bat her eyelashes and coo. The whole thing made Cassie sick.

"Cassie!" cried a friendly voice from a few feet

in front of her. Cassie's head turned, and a grin broke across her face.

"Melinda!" Cassie jumped to her feet to hug her best friend.

"It's so good to see you! How was your summer?"

"It was okay," said Cassie. "How was camp?"

"Great. It was really great," said Melinda. She gave Cassie another hug. Then she looked at her friend's muddy sneakers and dusty clothes.

"Cassie, what were you doing in the bushes?" she asked.

Cassie smiled. "Spying, of course. My parents finally bought me that Super Deluxe Spy Kit! I've been waiting for you to get home so we can spy together."

"Oh," said Melinda. "Well . . ." Her voice trailed off.

"Don't you have your kit anymore?" asked Cassie. "Don't tell me you lost it!"

"No, I didn't lose it. It's just that . . ."

It was at that moment that Cassie realized Melinda was wearing a skirt—a brightly colored, flared-out skirt. With paisley leggings underneath.

"You're wearing a skirt!" Cassie practically shouted at her friend. "And leggings!"

"I know. Doesn't it look pretty?"

"I guess so. But *why* are you wearing it?"

"What do you mean?" asked Melinda, looking insulted.

"I mean I've never seen you in a skirt before."

Marilee Tischler suddenly reappeared beside Melinda. "There you are!" she cried.

Cassie looked at the two girls standing together and felt her heart plunge into her stomach. They looked like twins.

"Did Melinda tell you we went to the same camp this summer?" said Marilee.

"No, she didn't," said Cassie, staring hard at her friend. Melinda squirmed uncomfortably.

Marilee smiled her snaky smile. "Are we still on for the mall this afternoon?" she asked Melinda sweetly.

Melinda nodded her head but said nothing.

Just then the school bell rang. Marilee grabbed Melinda's arm and led her into the crowd of students entering the school. Cassie dusted off her jeans, stuck the binoculars back in her spy belt, and swallowed the lump in her throat. Fifth grade had begun.

It was a terrible day. Cassie could hardly pay attention in her classes, and at lunch she sat alone while Melinda ate with the buzzing crowd around Marilee. The only good thing Cassie heard all day was the announcement about the first field trip of the year, to the local chapter of the National Weather Bureau. That sounded like fun. Cassie loved field trips. She liked any excuse to get out of school.

4

At the end of the day, while everyone was putting on their coats, Cassie attached the listening device from her Super Deluxe Spy Kit to Marilee's book bag. She wanted to hear just what kind of awful things Marilee was telling Melinda about her. And for Super Sleuth Cassie Williams, spying was the best way to discover anything.

Cassie hurried out of the building and headed straight for the bicycle rack. As usual, the class bully, Ben O'Brien, was snarling at a smaller kid, threatening to beat him up. Cassie ignored them.

She jumped on her bicycle and rode to Marilee's house, where she hid behind a row of trees across the street. She knew she wouldn't have to wait long. Marilee lived so close to school that she always walked home.

Sure enough, less than ten minutes later, Marilee, Melinda, and Stephanie Harrison strolled into hearing range. Cassie heard the crackle of static in her headphones and then voices.

"I mean, honestly, Melinda," Cassie heard Marilee say. "She just isn't growing up as fast as the rest of us."

"Maybe we're just growing up faster than everyone else," Melinda said softly.

"And that's exactly why we have to stick together," said Marilee. "Right, Stephanie?"

"Uh, yeah," said Stephanie.

"Cassie's really a lot of fun," said Melinda.

"Look, Melinda, you're going to have to

make a choice. Her or us!" said Marilee.

Cassie strained to hear Melinda's answer, but just then a large truck passed between Cassie and the group of girls, and the sound was lost. When Cassie picked up their voices again, they were talking about going to the mall after a snack at Marilee's.

Cassie waited, but the conversation stayed with shopping. She had just decided to go home when she heard something that made her gasp.

"Hey, Marilee," said Stephanie. "I like the pin on your book bag."

"What pin?" said Marilee.

"This one," Cassie heard Stephanie say. Then a sharp whine echoed through Cassie's ears as Stephanie picked at the listening device.

Cassie leaned out from behind the tree and saw that Stephanie had removed the microphone and was handing it to Marilee.

"Oh no!" cried Melinda. "Let me see that." Cassie held her breath as she watched and listened.

Marilee handed the device to Melinda, who turned it over in her hand and examined it. After a moment, she sighed and handed it back to Marilee.

"This is from the Super Deluxe Spy Kit," she said. "It's a microphone."

"Are you sure?" asked Stephanie.

"Of course I'm sure," said Melinda. "I have . . . I mean, I used to have one."

The next voice Cassie heard was Marilee's, loud and clear.

"Now listen here, Cassie Williams. We know you're on the other end of this. Get your own friends and stop spying on us. OR YOU'LL BE SORRY!"

With that, Marilee threw the microphone onto the driveway, and the three girls entered the house.

CHAPTER 2

All in all, it was a crummy week. After the humiliation of Monday, Cassie made an effort to keep her spying to a minimum. In fact, aside from the day she hid in a bathroom stall and eavesdropped on one of Marilee and Melinda's stupid conversations about clothes, Cassie didn't spy for four whole days.

But when she returned home from school on Friday afternoon, Cassie found someone else had taken up spying. Her little brother, Simon, was sitting on the floor of her bedroom, the contents of the Super Deluxe Spy Kit spread out around him.

"Simon!" Cassie cried when she saw him. "What are you doing? I told you not to touch my things!"

The small boy looked up.

"Show-and-tell, Cass," he said. He held up the night-vision periscope that he clutched in his tiny hand.

Simon had started kindergarten that week. As far as Cassie knew, this was her brother's very first homework assignment.

"Look, Simon," she said as nicely as she could. "Show-and-tell means to show and to tell about something that's yours. It doesn't mean you can just take something that doesn't belong to you."

"But you aren't using your spy kit anymore," Simon said, matter-of-factly. "And it's only for one day."

Cassie had to smile at her brother's logic. Simon was definitely the smartest five year old she had ever met. He had started talking when he was only a year old. Of course, so had Cassie. Mr. Williams was a language professor at the local university and had taught both of his children to read and write before most of the other children in the neighborhood had even picked up a book.

"So? Can I take the periscope?" asked Simon.

Cassie studied her brother's eager face for a moment. "No," she said. "I haven't even tried it out myself yet."

"But . . ."

"Now wait a minute, Simon. I said you can't take the periscope. But how about the finger-printing powder? There's a lot of it, and I'll show you how to use it. How would that be?"

Simon jumped up from the floor and threw his short arms around his sister.

"Thanks, Cass!" Simon looked so excited that

for a moment, Cassie thought maybe spying *should* be left to little kids—just like Marilee said. She sighed and stood up.

"No problem."

In the kitchen, Cassie showed her little brother how to dust drinking glasses for prints. Simon made a mess of things—he dropped a glass and spilled the white powder. And unfortunately, Mrs. Williams thought the glasses were just dirty and washed the powder off before dinner. But Simon's giggling reminded Cassie how much fun her Super Deluxe Spy Kit could be. The urge to spy was upon her again.

That evening, she decided to use the night-vision periscope. A cross between a submarine periscope and a telescope, it had a clamp for a ledge or windowsill. Just what made it a special night-vision periscope, Cassie couldn't say. But since it was nighttime, she thought she'd give it a try.

Cassie pulled up her window screen so she wouldn't have to look at the world through wire. After clamping the periscope to her sill, she knelt down and peered out.

At first she saw nothing but blackness. Then she realized that the periscope was aimed at a large tree on her neighbor's lawn. She tried to angle the instrument so she could see through the lit windows of the house. But no one was inside, and Cassie could barely make out the furniture. In the end, the only thing she could see clearly was the stars. That was okay with her. She had always loved the stars. All of her favorite books and movies that weren't about spying were about people traveling to distant planets.

Cassie stared at the night sky for about an hour and then went downstairs to say good night to her parents. When both her mother and father followed her back upstairs to tuck her in, Cassie wondered if Marilee would think this was a childish thing, too.

At three o'clock in the morning, Cassie woke in a sweat. She had just had the most horrible nightmare. Everyone in the fifth grade—Melinda, Marilee Tischler, and even Ben O'Brien—belonged to a private club. Cassie wandered from person to person, trying to find out what the name of the club was, who the members were, and why she couldn't join. But no one would answer her questions. No one would talk to her at all. So late one night, she found the clubhouse and used her flashlight to read the sign on the clubhouse door. In bold red letters it said: *Enemies of Cassie Williams.*

That was when she woke up. Cassie was so relieved to find she had been dreaming that she laughed out loud. She slipped out of bed and went to the bathroom, where she washed her face and drank a glass of water. Before sliding back into bed, Cassie decided to look at the stars again. She knelt down before her periscope and peered into the night.

And then she gasped. A silvery globe was plummeting from the sky. Faster and faster, it plunged downward. Cassie rubbed her eyes and looked again.

The globe grew larger as it spiraled toward earth, until suddenly it filled the whole lens of the periscope. Cassie leapt back and looked straight out the window. She watched as the shimmering ball crashed into a field right outside of town.

With that, Super Sleuth Cassie Williams sprang into action. She wasn't afraid. She knew just what to do.

CHAPTER

3

With the belt from her spy kit wrapped tightly around her waist, Cassie rode her bicycle across town. When she reached the open field that marked the edge of Hillsdale, she pedaled furiously over the grassy mounds and rocky ridges, shivering in the chill September air. Her heart was pounding. This was the most exciting thing that had ever happened to her. It was probably the most exciting thing in all of Hillsdale's long history.

Cassie's mind raced as fast as her feet pedaled. She made a mental checklist of all the gadgets she had brought. Night-vision periscope, check. Fingerprinting kit, check. Decoder, check. Listening device, check. Walkie-talkies, check.

Of course, Cassie wasn't really sure just what was waiting for her in the field outside of town. She wasn't even sure if that was where the silver globe had landed. And what *was* the silver globe? Was it a spaceship with aliens? Friendly aliens? Or maybe unfriendly ones—here to take over the earth!

Five minutes later, she saw it. The silver orb loomed in the field ahead. Cassie pedaled faster, her heart racing. Soon she could see the moonlight dancing off a series of rounded panels. If this wasn't a spaceship, what was it?

Ten feet from the globe, Cassie got off her bicycle and hid it behind a small stand of trees. As she dug in her spy belt for the periscope, only one thought filled her head—she should have left her parents a note. What if this *was* a spaceship and there *were* aliens aboard and they captured her and took her back to their planet? Or what if they were friendly and invited her for a visit? Yes, she definitely should have left a note.

> Spaceship landed.
> Went to check it out.
> Back soon,
>> Cassie

Or maybe,

> Went to a friend's house.
> On another planet.
> Love,
>> Cassie

The ship was silent, glistening in the light of

the moon. Cassie watched and waited, waited and watched. But nothing happened. Nothing at all. Was she dreaming? The tickle of a bug on her arm gave Cassie an immediate answer. In one expert motion, she squashed the mosquito before it had a chance to bite.

Cassie took a deep breath and stood up. A *real* spy would try to touch the ship, she told herself. She walked out of the bushes and into the open field.

The ship wasn't *silver* at all. It only looked that way in the moonlight. It was a deep golden color and seemed to be made entirely of long, rounded panels. Carefully, Cassie put a finger, and then her whole hand, against the nearest one. The ship felt smooth and warm. Cassie's hand tingled. For a moment, she thought about knocking. Maybe someone would come out. Or some*thing*.

Cassie's mouth was suddenly very dry. Her legs shaking, she turned and raced back to the trees.

For a moment, Cassie considered going home and waking her parents. But only for a moment. This was *her* discovery, *her* adventure! Suddenly Cassie was angry with herself. Why was she acting like a scared little kid? She was in fifth grade now. She was Cassie Williams, Super Sleuth. She knew what she had to do.

Cassie removed the magnetized long-range microphone from her spy belt and, clutching it in a moist hand, moved out into the field once more. She walked quickly to the ship, slipped the earphones on, and attached the microphone to a golden panel.

Then she listened.

At first there was only static. Then, slowly, another sound began to fill Cassie's ears. She tried to make some sense out of what she heard. But a strange clicking sound kept getting in the way. The more she listened, though, the more it seemed as if the clicks were supposed to be there, as if they were a part of some kind of mysterious language. Could these be alien voices?

Cassie had heard a lot of different languages spoken in her life. Her father spoke at least six fluently. But she had never heard a language with this clickety-click rhythm before. If the aliens sounded like this, what did they look like?

Just then Cassie heard a whirring sound, and slowly, two of the spaceship's panels began to separate. She grabbed the microphone and leapt back. Her eyes darted to the trees. She wanted to make the dash to safety, but suddenly her legs were locked. From between the open panels a small staircase emerged and lowered to the ground. Cassie looked to the top and found herself staring—at a hairless, completely green boy.

CHAPTER 4

The creature stared down at Cassie. Cassie stared back. As she watched, the alien reached out an arm and curled its fingernails—which were hooked and at least a foot in length—around the railing of the staircase. Then slowly the creature descended, step by step.

Cassie couldn't tear her eyes away. She knew she should do something: run or scream or speak. But she could only stand glued to the ground. She didn't know quite why she was so scared, though. The creature looked just like a human boy, or he would have if his skin wasn't green. And if he had hair. And if his fingernails were a foot shorter!

The alien reached the bottom of the staircase, stepped onto the ground, and raised both hands in a palms-up gesture. Cassie wondered if it was some form of greeting.

Suddenly the creature shot into the air. And just as suddenly he stopped. He floated four feet above the ground, shrieking in his clickety-click language.

Cassie had no idea what the alien was saying. But she was pretty sure he was calling for help—which was probably what she should be doing, if only she could find her voice.

A moment later, a larger creature appeared at the entrance to the ship. The smaller one seemed to calm down, though he continued to click in whatever language it was. The larger one responded and disappeared inside the ship. When he returned, he had a rope draped across his long, thick fingernails. In one skillful motion, he lassoed the smaller creature and brought him down to the ground. Both aliens then climbed back inside, leaving Cassie alone in the field below.

Now's your chance, Cassie told herself. Run for help. Run for your life. But something deep inside told Cassie this was not what she wanted to do. Scared as she was, she was still Cassie Williams, Super Sleuth, and what better opportunity for spying could there be? A real spaceship—with real live aliens! Cassie took a deep breath and raced for the safety of the trees.

From her hiding place, Cassie watched as the aliens reappeared at the top of the staircase. There were three of them now—the large green one, the small green one, and yet another that looked like a female. They were all dressed in form-fitting green clothes, only a shade or two darker than their skin. As they descended the staircase, Cassie noticed that each of them held a small metal device in the palm of his or her right hand.

Cassie was relieved to see that none of the creatures became airborne when they reached the ground. But they seemed confused and stood clicking among themselves, the small one gesturing to the spot where Cassie had stood. Finally, they separated, and Cassie watched as they searched the area around the ship, occasionally calling out in their strange language.

With a jolt Cassie realized that they were looking for her! Just as she was trying to decide what to do, the small one suddenly appeared in front of her, staring into the trees.

Cassie stood up.

The creature stepped back and called out to the others, who joined him. The three of them stood in a line, examining Cassie. When she stepped out of the trees, they moved back as one.

Stretching her lips awkwardly, Cassie managed a sort-of smile.

The female seemed to smile back.

At last Cassie found her voice. "Welcome to planet Earth," she croaked. She knew how stupid that sounded. But she also knew the aliens wouldn't understand her.

Upon hearing her voice, though, the creatures

started clicking and pointing, and then, unexpectedly, laughing. Cassie was stunned and relieved. At least their laughter sounded familiar. The smaller one parted his lips.

"You speak the language of the planet Quezon!" he exclaimed.

Cassie's mouth dropped open.

"Wha . . . ?" she said.

"You did say this is the planet Earth, did you not?" asked the larger creature.

"Uh, yes," Cassie stammered. She swallowed hard and spoke again. "We call this language English."

"English," said the large alien, rolling the word around on his tongue. "Interesting. I am Mirac from the planet Triminica."

"Um, I am Cassie from the planet Earth."

"Earth," repeated Mirac.

"Earth," said a mechanical voice from the top of the staircase. "A small class-R planet in the Milky Way galaxy." Cassie looked up and gasped. She was staring at an incredibly ugly creature made of blue metallic coils.

"What is *that*?" Cassie whispered.

The creature called Mirac glanced up at the staircase.

"Robot, I told you to remain inside the ship."

"*That* is a robot?" said Cassie. It was the strangest-looking robot she had ever seen. Not that she had seen many robots. Only the ones in movies.

"Go inside!" Mirac ordered.

"No," said Cassie, suddenly feeling very brave. "I'd like to meet him."

"Very well," said Mirac. "Descend, Robot, and meet the Earth creature."

The robot moved clumsily down the staircase and stood in front of Cassie. She found herself staring into huge, bulging eye sockets that had no eyes.

"So you're a robot!"

"Yes. And you are a higher Earth life-form called a human," the robot droned. "Humans are similar in appearance to Triminicans but with hair on their bodies."

"Hair?" asked Mirac.

"A keratin-based outgrowth covering the skin of some Earth mammals," the mechanical voice said. Cassie's hand flew up to her hair.

The robot continued. "In addition, humans lack sufficient keratin growth in the fingernail region."

Lack? thought Cassie, looking at the long, thick, curled fingernails of the aliens. By her way of thinking, she didn't have too little; *they* had too much.

"Hair and fingernails aren't the only differences between us," she blurted. "I mean, in case you haven't noticed—you're green!"

"What we have noticed is that *you* are not green!" said the smallest of the aliens, the one who had first appeared in the entrance to the ship. The more Cassie looked at him, the more she thought that if he had hair, clipped those fingernails, and was a different color, he might look like a boy in her school.

"Why should *I* be green?" Cassie asked him.

"We were informed that humans were green in color," he said, moving toward Cassie and staring intently at her.

"By whom?" asked Cassie, squirming a bit under his gaze.

"By I," said the robot.

"By me," said Cassie, automatically.

"By you?" said the mechanical voice.

"No, *you*. I mean, that is . . . I was just correcting your grammar," said Cassie. "I don't know how they speak English on that other planet. But here the correct phrase is 'by me,' not 'by I.'"

The large one laughed and said something in the clickety-click language. The small one responded. Back and forth they talked until Cassie couldn't stand it anymore. Suddenly she was no longer scared.

"Excuse me!" she said. And when they ignored her, she said it louder. "EXCUSE ME!"

The aliens stopped clicking and looked at her.

"What are you talking about?" she asked.

Looks were exchanged all around. Cassie knew those looks well. They were the kind of secretive glances adults gave each other when they

24

were trying to decide whether or not to trust her with a piece of information.

Finally, the smaller alien spoke.

"The robot has many functions. One is the ability to access the ship's computer banks in order to determine any pertinent information we need to assimilate into a new culture. We were simply discussing the fact that not all the information supplied by our computer banks appears to have been correct."

"Wow!" said Cassie. "How old are you?"

"I fail to see the correlation between my last statement and your question," the small one said, studying Cassie carefully as he spoke.

"Just answer the question, please," said Cassie.

The mechanical voice jumped in. "He is the equivalent of ten of your Earth years."

"I thought so," said Cassie. "That's how old I am."

"Then what precisely is the problem?" demanded the small one.

Cassie grinned. "No problem," she said. "It's just that you have an excellent command of the English language. Most kids our age don't use all those big words."

The creature just stared at her. His eyes sparkled a startling shade of green, almost the same color as his skin.

"It was a compliment," said Cassie.

The alien relaxed and smiled. Then he leaned

over and said something to the robot. The robot responded. The alien looked at Cassie.

"Would you care to come aboard for a . . . scotch?" he asked.

Cassie stared, then had to giggle. "Ten-year-old earthlings don't drink scotch. But I would love to come aboard."

Her legs didn't start shaking again until the golden doors sealed shut behind them.

CHAPTER

The inside of the spaceship was bathed in a golden light. A control panel arced halfway around the room. In the middle of the floor, a clear tubelike structure housed a fiery red liquid that spit and bubbled and popped.

Cassie walked toward the control panel but found the robot blocking her path.

"Let us linger in here," said Mirac, gently taking Cassie's arm with two fingernails and leading her through an archway into another room.

Cushions of light hovered against the rounded walls of the room. The small creature settled himself on one, placing the small metal device he was holding on a table next to him. Mirac gestured for Cassie to sit down. She put out a hand and gently touched a thick cloud of dull light. It felt firm and warm and comforting, like a favorite old chair. Cassie jumped up onto it and grinned.

Just then the female appeared with what looked to Cassie like pieces of wet cloth. She

handed one to each of the male creatures and then left the room. Mirac spread the cloth across his fingernails, brought it up to his face, and scrubbed.

Cassie gasped. Mirac's skin was now the same color as hers, while the cloth was soaked in green. Cassie looked over at the smaller alien— and found herself staring at what looked like a hairless Earth boy.

"Face paint," said the alien. Then he grinned. Cassie couldn't believe it. He was cute!

"We wanted to fit in," Mirac explained.

"If you had hair, you would look just like us," said Cassie.

"If you didn't, you would look like us," said the female, entering the room. She was no longer green either.

Everyone settled on a cloud of light, and the robot served them a liquid Cassie couldn't identify. She waited until the aliens had drunk from their glasses before sipping from her own. It tasted like a fizzy version of melted Jell-O.

"What is your name?" Cassie asked the smallest of the aliens.

"I am Zekephlon," he said formally, pronouncing the name with a lot of clicks. "This is Mirac and Inora. They are my . . ." The boy paused as if he were searching for the correct word.

"Parents," droned the robot.

"As I said, we are from the planet Triminica,"

Mirac explained. "We were heading for our vacation destination on the planet Clurigan when our ship's computers malfunctioned."

"And you landed on Earth!" said Cassie.

"Exactly."

"Tell us about Earth," said Zekephlon, leaning forward eagerly.

"There is plenty of time for that," his father said gently. "This Earth creature has many questions. We will answer them first. Then she will answer ours."

"Please call me Cassie," said Cassie.

"Very well, Cassie. What would you like to know?"

Cassie tried to form only one question in her head. But when she spoke, they all tumbled out at once. "Well, for one thing, have you been here before? Have any aliens been here before? Did you know about Earth before you landed? What is that strange language you speak?" She pointed at Zekephlon. "And why did he float up into the air before?"

"One question at a time," Mirac said, laughing.

Cassie blushed, then grinned.

"No, *we* have not been here before," said Mirac. "Actually, I do not believe anyone from our world has been to this galaxy before. As far as language is concerned, we speak Triminican. But we are also fluent in the languages of all of the planets in our solar system."

30

"We speak many languages on this planet," said Cassie.

"Interesting," said Mirac. "And do you all speak all of the languages?"

"No," said Cassie. "I mean, some people speak more languages than others. But I'm not sure anyone can speak them all. Not even my father."

Cassie's eyes fell upon the small metal device sitting on the table.

"What's that?" she asked.

"It is a gravitonizer," said Mirac. "It grounds us when we are on a planet with an inferior gravity pull."

"So that's why you floated off the ground!" Cassie exclaimed.

"Yes," Zekephlon nodded. "We must wear our gravitonizers on this planet at all times."

Zekephlon leaned toward Cassie, his green eyes glistening.

"What was the device *you* were using when I first departed this vessel?" he asked.

"Zekephlon, I said our questions will come later," Mirac said sternly.

"That's okay," said Cassie. She smiled at the boy. "It's from my Super Deluxe Spy Kit," she said.

"Spy kit?" Zekephlon jumped off the chair. "Are you a spy?"

"Not a real one," said Cassie. "It's just a toy."

"I am a student at the Interstellar Spy

Academy," the boy announced proudly.

"No kidding?" asked Cassie. "Wow. What is that, exactly?"

"I am in training to be a spy. When I grow up, I will ride the great starships on secret missions."

"Wow!" Cassie said again.

"And you wish to be a spy, also?" Zekephlon looked at her eagerly.

Cassie couldn't believe it. She had finally found someone who would spy with her. So what if he was an alien? So what if she couldn't pronounce his name? She didn't think she was in a position to be picky about friends right now. She found herself smiling at the small alien. After a moment, he grinned back.

Cassie and the Triminicans talked for hours. They spoke a little about Earth and a little about Triminica. But mostly they talked about being stranded on a strange planet with a broken spaceship.

"How will the members of your planet treat us?" Mirac asked. "Will we be welcome?"

Cassie took a deep breath. "I don't really know," she said. "We've never had visitors from another planet here."

"Really?" said Mirac. "Never?"

He stood up and stretched his large frame. Then he linked his hands behind his back and began pacing. He reminded Cassie of her father.

32

"Video-viewing entertainment shows cruel treatment to those from outside Earth," droned the robot. "These earthlings are our enemies and wish to rule our planet and all planets."

"Is this true?" asked Inora.

"He's talking about movies," said Cassie. "But, yes, it is true. In most of the movies made about spaceships landing on earth, the aliens are experimented on and kept in cages and . . ." Cassie's voice trailed off. Suddenly, she felt guilty. That had always been her favorite kind of movie.

"Many years ago, we did cruel things to new beings that landed on our planet," said Mirac. "We did it in the name of science."

"Well, that's what would happen here," said Cassie.

Mirac sighed. "I believe that with the robot's assistance I can repair the damaged areas of the ship. But we lack the necessary raw materials to make enough fuel to return home."

"Is there no one on your planet who would help us locate these elements?" Zekephlon asked Cassie.

"I don't think so, Zeke," said Cassie. "You don't mind if I call you Zeke, do you?"

Zekephlon grinned. "I like it!"

A silence settled over the ship. There seemed to be nothing else to say. Finally, Mirac spoke.

"Then it is settled," he said. "We will search for

the raw materials ourselves. Cassie, do you know a place named Hawaii?"

"Sure," said Cassie. "But it's really far away from here."

"But it is on this planet?" asked Mirac.

"Yes."

"Then that is where we must go. The robot tells me that the main ingredient for our fuel, iridium, is located in a part of this Hawaii called a volcano."

"You can't go into a volcano!" Cassie cried.

"We have no other choice," said Mirac. "Inora, you will come with me. The robot will look after Zekephlon and guard the ship."

The robot started to object. Mirac silenced it with a look.

Cassie studied the aliens. They seemed so much like any happy family that suddenly she couldn't bear the thought of what might happen to them if they were discovered. If only they had hair, if only their fingernails weren't long and curled, if only they weren't wearing those strange one-piece uniforms, they might pass as humans.

Suddenly Cassie knew just what to do.

CHAPTER

6

"It's woof woof or arf arf," Cassie explained again. "Those are your only choices."

"Come on, Robot. Try again," Zeke urged.

"I fail to see why this is necessary," said the mechanical voice.

"We've already explained this," said Zeke. "You are to assume the appearance of an Earth dog in order to blend in on this planet. Do you want me to get Mirac and have him explain it to you again?"

"That is not necessary," said the robot quickly.

"Then try it again," said Zeke. "Woof woof or arf arf."

"And get down on all fours," said Cassie.

"It is not enough that I have to be covered with this keratin growth. Now I have to move around like an animal." The mechanical voice was growing louder and snippier.

Cassie looked at the robot and tried hard not to laugh. She had glued a dozen wigs to his metallic body. He looked like some strange sort of sheepdog. An ugly, undersized sheepdog with no eyes and a huge head. He looked ridiculous. But it was all part of the plan that had evolved in the wee hours of the morning.

The plan was in four steps: Cassie would help the Triminicans to look like Earth creatures; the Triminicans would hide their spaceship; Zeke would enroll in Hillsdale Elementary School so he would not only blend in, but learn about Earth as well; and Mirac and Inora would go to Hawaii.

Of course, hiding the spaceship was going to be a challenge, because its invisibility shield had been damaged in the crash. And although Mirac insisted that mining iridium from a volcano in Hawaii would be the same as mining corengi from the craters of Triminica's second moon, Cassie had her doubts. The part that had concerned Cassie the most, though, was money. How was she going to purchase all the necessary supplies? How would Zeke pay for schoolbooks and food and clothes? How would Mirac and Inora get around Hawaii?

But when she had voiced these fears to the Triminicans the night before, Inora had simply disappeared into another section of the ship. When she reappeared a few minutes later, she handed Cassie a small canvas bag that was unusually heavy.

"The robot tells me these may be valuable on your planet," Inora explained.

Cassie opened the small bag and gasped. It was packed with solid gold hoops.

It turned out that the main export of Triminica was gold. In the Triminicans' galaxy, gold was not used for making jewelry. It was used for building houses and starships and gadgets that Cassie had never even dreamed of. Gadgets such as gravitonizers and materializers and tractor-beam ray guns.

So that morning, while the aliens puzzled over the dilemma of where and how to hide the ship, Cassie was at the Hillsdale Mall, shopping with money the jeweler had paid her for the gold hoops.

Now it was afternoon. Cassie had returned to the ship with the supplies and gone straight to work on the robot.

"Try it again," said Zeke.

"Woof," said the robot, mechanically.

Cassie sighed. "He needs a dog name," she said.

"What about . . . Lassie?" said the robot.

"What?" Cassie laughed.

"That is the name of your most famous dog, is it not? Why can I not have a famous name?" The robot sounded almost hurt.

Cassie looked at Zeke. "Does this robot have feelings?" she asked.

"Of course I have feelings," said the mechanical voice.

"Simulated feelings," Zeke explained.

"Sorry," said Cassie. "I didn't know."

"There is much you do not know," said the robot.

"I said I was sorry—SPOT!" shouted Cassie.

Zeke laughed and stood up. "Okay," he said. "Spot it is."

"Now it's your turn!" Cassie said, turning to Zeke. She had bought him a short brown wig with bangs. The alien sat on one of the clouds of light while his new Earth friend fitted the wig to his head and combed the bangs down over his forehead with her fingers. Cassie had to admit that Zeke looked really cute. But more important, he looked human. The jeans and shirts she had bought for him would complete the picture.

But first—the fingernails. Cassie reached into a bag and pulled out a pair of clippers and an emery board.

"You have to cut your fingernails," she told Zeke.

"But they are necessary for so many actions," the alien protested.

"I've been watching you," said Cassie. "You use your nails for the same things we use our fingers for. You'll just have to get used to using your fingers, too!"

Zeke gazed longingly at his hands.

"Think of it as a spy mission," said Cassie. "You have to assume an alien's identity."

Zeke's face lit up.

Cassie reached for another bag. "I bought you a present," she said, pulling a box out of the bag and handing it to Zeke. "It's a Super Deluxe Spy Kit! I have one just like it. I know it's just an Earth toy, and you're a real spy . . ."

"I like it very much," said Zeke, smiling and opening the box.

Cassie helped Zeke to fit all the spy devices into the belt. Then the two spies went in search of Mirac and Inora. The most difficult task was still ahead.

"Spot has calculated that we will need seventeen materializer disks," Zeke told Cassie.

"Is that good?" asked Cassie.

"It is neither good nor bad. It just is," said Spot's voice from beneath a mass of hair. He was standing upright. Cassie thought he looked like a dark-haired abominable snowman.

"One disk is usually used to transport from one to ten persons," Zeke explained. "We have never attempted to move an entire spaceship this way."

"Where are you moving it?" asked Cassie.

"There is a small clearing in the forest on the other side of this field," said Zeke. "Mirac has the coordinates."

"It is time!" Mirac announced. He bent down and picked up a box from the ground. Then he plucked the first materializer disk out of the box. It was flat, round, and golden.

"Are the coordinates set on each disk?" Mirac asked the robot.

"Affirmative," said Spot.

Mirac threw the first disk. It arched high and wide in the sky, then headed straight for the ship. At the exact moment Cassie thought the two would collide, the disk spun outward and began to circle the ship, slowly at first, and then faster and faster. Ring after ring of sparkling light trailed after the disk.

Mirac threw another disk and another and another. Each one followed the path the first one had taken, spinning furiously around the ship. Each left in its path a thin stream of light. By the time Mirac threw the seventeenth disk, the sky was ablaze with sparkling vapors.

And then suddenly, the ship was gone.

"It worked!" cried Zeke.

"We will see," said Mirac. "Zekephlon, you take Cassie. Inora and the robot and I will travel together."

"Ready?" Zeke asked Cassie. Pulling a materializer disk from his shoe, he punched at the tiny flickering buttons. Before Cassie could say a word, Zeke reached for her hand and threw the disk. It boomeranged back and began to circle them. Ring after ring of sparkles surrounded the friends, spinning faster and faster until Cassie had to close her eyes to keep from getting dizzy. As she felt her feet leave the ground, Cassie realized that this was the first time she had ever held hands with a boy.

They materialized in the forest clearing and immediately saw the ship. Mirac, Inora, and Spot appeared a moment later, and everyone set about covering the ship with branches and leaves.

By the time they finished, the sun was setting. It was time for Cassie to go home, for Mirac and Inora to start their journey, and for the spy from outer space to start his life as an earthling boy.

CHAPTER

On Monday morning Cassie went to social studies class and forgot the main exports of Australia. From there she went to science class, where she blew up her experiment. In French class she couldn't conjugate the verb *vouloir.* Keeping her alien friends a secret and not flunking out of school were going to be hard to do at the same time.

But somehow Cassie didn't even mind not having anyone to eat with in the cafeteria. The day after tomorrow that would all change. Early that morning Cassie had explained to the principal that Zeke was her cousin, whose family was moving to Hillsdale, and who would be staying with her until his parents arrived and his new house was ready. It took only ten minutes of whining and begging before the principal agreed to put Zeke in all of Cassie's classes.

When the last bell of the day rang, Cassie ran the whole way to the spaceship. The ship was hidden a long distance from the school, and she was exhausted by the time she got there. Zeke served her a snack of something she couldn't identify, and they quizzed Spot on his woofs and arfs. Then Cassie said that she had to be getting home.

Zeke looked so sad and lonely that Cassie couldn't stand it.

"Why don't you come over to my house?" she asked.

"Absolutely not," the robot answered for him.

"Oh, come on, Spot," said Cassie. "What's the problem? I'll just tell my parents that he's a new friend I made in school. He can stay for a little while and then come right back."

"No," said Spot stubbornly.

"Yes," said Zeke. "I would like that very much."

"Mirac will be angry," said Spot.

"Mirac is not here," said Zeke. "I will be back in time to eat the next meal."

Cassie and Zeke raced for the door of the spaceship. Once outside, they used a materializer to disappear before Spot could say another word.

Cassie curled up on her bed and watched Zeke. He was walking around the room, practicing picking things up with his fingers.

Suddenly Cassie had a thought. "Can you fly?" she asked.

"No," said Zeke. "Can you?"

Cassie shook her head and chewed on a pencil thoughtfully. "Have you *tried* to fly since you landed on Earth?"

"Why should I?"

"Well, for one thing, you were pretty close to flying the first time I saw you," said Cassie. "And everyone knows that when you land on a foreign planet, you develop superpowers."

"Superpowers?"

"Yeah. Like Superman. Can you bend steel?"

"Steel?"

"Maybe you have X-ray vision." Cassie jumped off the bed and grabbed a suitcase from a corner of the room.

"What's in here?" she asked Zeke, holding it up.

"I do not know. Open it," said Zeke.

"No, Zeke. Concentrate. Try to see through the suitcase."

Zeke stared at the suitcase for a moment, squinting his eyes. Then he shrugged his shoulders.

"Sorry, Cassie. I do not think I have any superpowers," he said.

"Well," said Cassie, disappointed. "Then, let's spy!"

"Absolutely!" said Zeke. "Who should we spy on?"

"How about my father? He's working in his study, and we aren't supposed to disturb him until dinner."

"I would very much like to spy on a male Earth being," said Zeke. "Let us begin." Zeke took three strides to the door and threw it open.

Super Sleuth Cassie Williams and her new spying partner crouched outside the Williamses' house, beneath the window of the ground-floor office. They each held the binoculars from their Super Deluxe Spy Kits.

"Ready?" whispered Cassie.

"Ready!" said Zeke.

Slowly Zeke rose up from his hunched position until his head was above the windowsill.

"I see him," whispered Zeke.

"Describe," said Cassie. She tried to sound brisk and official.

"A male Earth being, sitting in front of a screen with green lettering of some sort," Zeke reported.

"That's a computer," Cassie explained.

Zeke stared into the window for another minute and then dropped down beside Cassie.

"This is most unsatisfactory," he said. "We are too close to use this device properly." Zeke held up the binoculars in his hand.

Cassie looked around the backyard of her house. Her face lit up as her eyes landed on the massive oak tree.

"Follow me," she whispered to Zeke.

Zeke was amazingly clumsy at climbing trees. But eventually he and Cassie made it to the top branch. Cassie didn't tell her new friend that she had spent many hours nestled in this tree, spying on neighbors. She wanted him to think it was a new adventure for them both.

Spying on Mr. Williams was not very interesting. He didn't do anything but type on his computer and look through books. But the Triminican loved the binoculars. He kept adjusting and readjusting them. He stared at the sky, he stared at the trees, then he leaned back and tried to look at Cassie through them.

"I'm bored," said Cassie. "We need someone better to spy on. Let's get down from here."

"You are correct," said Zeke. "But I must have one more opportunity to look through these wonderful spyglasses." He raised them to his eyes again and surveyed the yard of Cassie's house.

Cassie laughed. "I can't believe a planet as advanced as yours doesn't have binoculars."

Then Zeke gasped. "Oh no!" he said. "Cassie, look!"

Cassie peered through her binoculars to the place where Zeke pointed. She found herself staring at a large furry object.

"Spot!" she cried.

"Arf," Spot called up to her.

The two spies scrambled down from the tree as fast as possible.

"Robot, what are you doing here?" Zeke asked.

"Zeke, there's no time for that," said Cassie, looking around to make sure no one could see them. "Get him out of here. I'll meet you at the ship before school tomorrow morning."

Zeke grabbed on to one of the wigs glued to Spot, then reached into his shoe and pulled out a materializer disk. He quickly punched coordinates into the device and threw the disk. As her new friends disappeared in a cloud of sparkling light, Cassie looked at the back door of her house. There stood Simon, his tiny mouth wide open, his eyes all aglow.

"Where'd you get the sparkles, Cass?" he said.

"Uh . . . um . . . it's a magic trick," said Cassie.

"Do it again!" said Simon, clapping his chubby hands together.

"I've got a better idea," said Cassie. "Let's go play with the fingerprinting powder."

"No," said Simon. "Sparkles."

Cassie studied Simon for a moment. There was only one way out of this situation, and she knew just what it was. Cassie sighed.

"I tell you what, Simon," she said. "If you stop talking about the sparkles—and that means not saying anything to Mom or Dad either—I'll let you take the periscope to show-and-tell next week."

"Really?"

"Really."

Simon thought about it.

"Okay," he finally said.

Cassie breathed a sigh of relief and followed her brother into the house. They went into the kitchen, where Cassie made a snack for both of them. Before biting into his sandwich, Simon smiled at Cassie and said, "Where'd you find that big fuzzy dog?"

CHAPTER 8

Spot was going to be a problem. He insisted on following Zeke everywhere. Hiding the materializers was useless. Spot didn't need them. His inbuilt system could record the coordinates Zeke set, and the robot could follow in his own time.

He woofed and he arfed. He crawled on all fours. But Spot looked more like a robot with wigs on than a dog. Especially if you looked at his eye sockets.

"Can't you program him to really think he's a dog?" Cassie asked as she and Zeke walked to school on Wednesday morning.

"I could," said Zeke. "But then he would not be any more help to me than a dog."

"So?" said Cassie.

"I might need him," said Zeke simply.

As they neared the entrance to the school, the alien stopped walking and turned toward Cassie. "I believe I am nervous," he said.

"Me, too," said Cassie.

"Why would you be nervous?"

"I don't want anyone to discover where you're from."

"Ah yes. You would also be in trouble, then, because you did not turn us in."

Cassie was silent. She didn't want to tell Zeke that he was the only new friend she had made since school started. She wanted him to think she was popular. She wanted him to like her more than anyone else he met. She looked up into Zeke's sparkling eyes and smiled.

"I guess that's the reason," she said.

"Woof," said Spot. Cassie looked down at the mangy mutt who wasn't even pretending not to follow them. He was trotting right next to Zeke and seemed to think he was going to school, too.

"You aren't behaving like a dog at all," said Cassie, exasperated. "You're supposed to wander away from us and sniff things."

"Sniff things?" said Spot.

"You know, smell bushes and grass and trees," said Cassie.

"I do not have a dog's sense of smell," said Spot.

Cassie rolled her eyes at Zeke.

"I think perhaps you should return to the ship now," Zeke said to the robot.

"I will attend school with you," said Spot.

"Absolutely not!" said Cassie. "Do you want to ruin everything? Dogs aren't allowed in school."

"Then I will wait outside the building," said Spot obstinately.

"Well . . ." Zeke sighed. "Be careful not to be seen."

"And keep your head down," said Cassie. "If someone does see you, at least don't let them see your face."

The schoolyard was overflowing with children and parents, cars and buses. Zeke was fascinated with the "primitive moving vehicles." But what caught his interest most were the kids arriving on skateboards and Rollerblades.

"That seems to be an inefficient mode of travel," said Zeke, pointing to a boy on a skateboard.

Cassie stopped walking and grabbed Zeke's arm. The alien turned to face her.

"Zeke, you can't talk like that in school," said Cassie.

"Like what?" asked Zeke.

"'Inefficient mode of travel,'" said Cassie, repeating Zeke's words.

"Why? Did I convey my thoughts improperly?"

"There! You did it again!" said Cassie. "Kids our age don't use words like *inefficient* and *mode* and *convey*."

"Why not?" asked Zeke.

Cassie sighed. "Well, for one thing, a lot of them don't know what those words mean," she explained. "For another thing, even the kids who know what those words mean wouldn't use them."

"What would they say?"

"Just use smaller words, okay?"

Zeke shrugged his shoulders. "It makes no sense, but it sounds satisfactory." He stopped and grinned. "I mean, okay."

"And for your information," said Cassie, "skateboards are not only a 'mode of travel.' They're fun!"

Zeke watched a boy glide to the school entrance, skid to a stop, flip up his skateboard, and catch it in midair.

"It does look like fun," Zeke admitted. "I would like to have one of those."

"Yeah?" said Cassie. "Maybe after school we'll go to the mall and buy you one."

"The mall?" said Zeke.

"You don't know what a mall is?" asked Cassie. "That does it. We're definitely going there after school today."

Cassie felt cheerful at the thought of the mall. But as they entered the building, her nervousness returned. There were so many things that could go wrong. What if Zeke's wig fell off? What if the gravitonizer fell out of his pocket? What if he knew so little of Earth subjects that he couldn't answer any questions at school?

Cassie was worrying about the wrong things. Zeke was a whiz in math class, and he spoke French fluently with the teacher. His English was so textbook perfect, the teacher overlooked that he had never heard of the books every fifth grader was supposed to have read. Soon Cassie was worrying that Zeke would be in college by the end of the week.

Yet another worry came up at lunchtime. In the crowded cafeteria, Cassie had a chance to compare Zeke to the other students. He was cuter than the other boys. Much cuter. His sparkling eyes and confident manner made him a magnet for every girl in the class who was even the slightest bit interested in boys. Which mostly meant Marilee Tischler.

Cassie and Zeke sat alone at a table while she taught him how to twirl spaghetti on a fork.

"Hi, Cassie," said Melinda. She was standing next to the table with Marilee and Stephanie. All eyes were on Zeke.

"Hi, Melinda," said Cassie.

"Mind if we sit with you?" asked Marilee as she sat down next to Zeke and smiled her sticky-sweetest smile at him.

Cassie introduced Zeke to everyone. When she mentioned that he was her cousin, Melinda's eyebrows raised. Cassie tried to remember if Melinda knew that both of her parents were only children. One more thing to worry about, she thought.

Marilee flirted with Zeke the entire lunch period. It wasn't the flirting that bothered Cassie so much. It was how much Zeke seemed to be enjoying it. It had never occurred to her that he might like girls in the way that boys on Earth liked girls. Especially since most of the boys in fifth grade at Hillsdale Elementary School were having trouble deciding if girls were more interesting than basketball or baseball or football.

When the lunch bell rang, everyone scrambled back to their homerooms to get their coats. Cassie had almost forgotten that this was the afternoon of the trip to the National Weather Bureau.

Three buses were waiting outside the school to take the entire fifth grade on the field trip. Laughing and talking, the children climbed on and took their seats. No one noticed the burly man tossing an odd-looking dog into a van labeled Dogcatcher.

CHAPTER 9

When they arrived at the weather bureau, the class was divided into four groups, each with a tour guide. Marilee and her friends trailed after Zeke and made sure they were put in the same group as the Triminican. Cassie felt completely ignored. And the many twists and turns in the corridors of the building made her feel like spying.

Her group was listening to a lecture on weather patterns and star charts when Cassie heard the sound of running feet behind her. She turned quickly and saw a man disappear down a flight of stairs.

"Zeke," she whispered to her friend. "Let's spy."

"On whom?" Zeke whispered back.

"I just saw a man run down those stairs back there. Let's follow him."

"Shhhh," said Marilee in her snottiest whisper. "Some of us are trying to listen."

"Zeke!" Cassie tugged on the alien's arm.

Zeke bent down and whispered in her ear, "Cassie, as much as I'd like to spy with you, I really don't think I should draw attention to myself right now."

Cassie knew Zeke was right. But she was bored with the lecture and burning up with curiosity about what was down those stairs. Quietly, she slipped away from the group and followed the path that the running man had taken.

When she reached the bottom of the stairs, Cassie heard voices coming out of a room to her right. She tiptoed to the open door and flattened her back against the wall. Then she listened.

"If it wasn't a meteorite, what was it?" said a woman's voice.

"That's what I'm trying to tell you, Kate," a man's voice said impatiently.

The woman sighed. "This is getting out of hand, Grant," she said. "Every time there's a meteor shower, you think we're being invaded by little green men."

"I didn't say they were green. And I didn't say they were little," said Grant.

"Very funny," said Kate.

"And there were five UFO reportings that night," said Grant.

"I'm going to tell you this for the last time, Grant. We are the weather bureau. We are not a branch of the UFO sightings service. You are a talented scientist. And usually your experiments are well grounded in fact. If you insist on spending your time searching for extraterrestrials, perhaps you should get a job at NASA."

Cassie heard a door slam shut. She took a deep breath and peered into the room. A tall man wearing wire-rimmed glasses stood alone, holding a stack of papers. The walls were lined with computers busily processing information, and there was a door at the back of the room. Cassie guessed that the woman had disappeared behind it.

The man turned around, and Cassie flattened her back against the wall so he wouldn't see her. Then the man raced abruptly out of the room and hustled down the hallway. She watched him run down the corridor and turn a corner.

While the rest of the fifth grade was learning about the Doppler tracking system, Cassie Williams, Super Sleuth, was running on her tiptoes after Grant Trexler. He slipped from one hallway into another and finally exited the building.

When Cassie burst through the door, she found herself outside, in a small lot packed with garbage cans and abandoned machinery. She couldn't see anyone, but she could hear the low murmur of voices. They were coming from the other side of a huge garbage Dumpster.

Swiftly and quietly, Cassie slipped behind the Dumpster. Then she listened.

"Why did you call?" Grant was saying.

"Like I was telling you," another man's voice said, "I remembered my brother-in-law sayin' how you was always lookin' for strange things that might be from another planet."

"Your brother-in-law has a big mouth," said Grant.

"Maybe so, maybe so," said the other man. "You interested in what I got to say or not?"

"How much is this going to cost me?" asked Grant.

"I'll tell you what I got, and you tell me how much it's worth," growled the man.

Just then something scurried over one of Cassie's feet, and before she could stop herself, she stumbled forward, banging into the Dumpster.

"Who's there?" Grant called out.

Cassie froze. Grant advanced toward the Dumpster and leaned over. Suddenly Cassie was looking into dark, menacing eyes. Eyes that were so dark, you could barely see the pupils.

"What are you doing here?" Grant snarled, reaching out and grabbing Cassie's arm.

Cassie yanked her arm out of Grant's grasp and was on her feet and running before she could think of anything else to do.

"Catch her!" she heard Grant yell to the other man.

The man jumped into Cassie's path, but she dodged him and dashed for the entrance to the building. As she ducked inside she heard the sound of thundering footsteps following her.

She was running so quickly that she didn't see Zeke coming toward her.

"Cassie!" Zeke cried out. "I've been looking all over for you."

"Run, Zeke! They're after us!"

"Who?"

But there was no time for Cassie to answer. "We've got to hide, Zeke," she said urgently.

Zeke's eyes scanned the hallways. Then suddenly, they lit up.

"Cassie, give me your hand," he said.

"Wha . . . ?"

Zeke reached out with one hand and grabbed Cassie by the shoulder. With the other hand he pulled the gravitonizer from his pocket and dropped it on the floor. A split second before Grant Trexler entered the corridor, Zeke and Cassie shot up into the air. They hovered just beneath the ceiling, their hearts in their throats, as Grant raced under them. He was moving so quickly that he didn't see the tiny device.

Cassie watched Grant disappear into another room and breathed a sigh of relief.

"What do we do now?" she whispered to Zeke.

"I'm going to let go," said Zeke. "Make sure to bend your knees when you land."

Zeke let go of Cassie's shoulder, and she crashed to the floor.

"Throw me the gravitonizer!" Zeke called down to her.

Cassie lunged for the small metal object and threw it up to Zeke. He caught it in his right hand and gently floated down to the floor. His feet hit the ground just as Grant Trexler appeared in the doorway at the end of the hall.

"There you are!" he snarled.

"Oh no!" cried Cassie. "He must have heard me fall!"

The two spies took off down the twisting hallways of the weather bureau, the scientist close on their heels. They saw an exit sign, opened the door, and hurried into the sunshine, where the rest of the fifth grade was boarding the buses for the trip back to school.

As Zeke and Cassie cut into line in front of Marilee and Melinda, Grant Trexler pushed open the exit door and stopped. From a window of the bus, Cassie watched the sunlight glinting off the scientist's glasses and shivered. Behind those glasses were the meanest eyes she had ever seen.

"Why was he following you?" Zeke whispered as he slid into the seat beside Cassie.

"I'm not really sure," Cassie whispered back. She leaned her head against the back of the seat and stared out the window, wondering.

As the bus pulled away, Cassie gave only a fleeting thought as to why a dogcatcher's van would be in the parking lot of the weather bureau.

CHAPTER

10

When the buses dropped them off in front of the school, Cassie and Zeke headed straight for the mall. While they walked, Cassie told Zeke about the conversations she had overheard.

"Strange," said Zeke. "What do you think it means?"

"I don't know," said Cassie. "But he made me very nervous. I mean, why was he so upset that I overheard him talking with that other man?"

"It doesn't matter," said Zeke. "He is no match for a student of the Interstellar Spy Academy."

"Zeke, this isn't a game. The guy was talking about capturing aliens."

"He will never catch me," said Zeke. "I am a trained spy."

Cassie groaned. She didn't know exactly what kind of spy training Zeke had, but she didn't see how a ten year old—from any planet—could out-wit an adult scientist.

"Besides," said Zeke. "You said he only *thought*

_s had landed on earth. You gave no indication at all that he thinks *I* am an alien."

"Hey, yeah!" said Cassie. But as they got closer to the mall, she was troubled by some nagging thoughts: maybe Grant didn't know that Zeke was an alien, but he had seen Cassie. Would he come after her? Would he recognize her if he saw her again? Would she accidentally lead that horrible man to Zeke? She would just have to wait. And Zeke would have to be careful—very, very careful.

Just inside the mall entrance, Zeke froze.

"What's wrong?" asked Cassie.

"What is this place?" asked the alien. His eyes were glistening more than usual, and a huge grin spread across his face.

"This," said Cassie, "is The Mall."

"What is its purpose?"

"Zeke, you're blocking the entrance. Let's go up to the fourth floor and have a soda. I'll explain the whole mall to you there."

The fourth floor was packed with teenagers and preteenagers and anyone else whose parents would let them go to the mall after school. Three walls were lined with food stands. In the center of the floor was a fountain. Cassie and Zeke found an empty table near it.

"So, what don't you understand about the mall?" Cassie asked as she took a sip of her chocolate ice-cream soda.

"I think I understand already," said Zeke. "It is a gathering place, correct?"

"Yeah. Sort of," said Cassie. She gestured around her. "At least, this part of the mall is for gathering. The rest of it is for shopping."

"I did not see food stores on the other floors," said Zeke.

"Not that kind of shopping. Clothes and toys and jewelry and furniture. That kind of stuff. Don't you go shopping on Triminica?"

"The robot shops for food," said Zeke.

"No kidding?" said Cassie. "So if I went to the supermarket on your planet, it would be me and a bunch of robots shopping?"

The color drained from Zeke's face.

"Zeke, what is it?" Cassie asked.

"The robot!" said Zeke. "We left him at school!"

"No we didn't," said Cassie. "I looked for him in the schoolyard as we were leaving. He wasn't there."

"Why did you not say anything?" asked Zeke.

"I figured he got bored and went back to the ship," said Cassie. "Just like you told him to do."

Zeke relaxed a bit. "Of course, you're probably right. Although I'm not sure that the robot gets bored."

"Never mind about Spot," said Cassie. "There's something I want to show you. Does Triminica have video arcades?"

"Hmmm," said Zeke. "Video arcades. I was learning about those on the ship's computer last night. They sound very similar to the revolving game planets of Seturnigan. Is there one in this mall?"

"There sure is!" said Cassie, standing up and pushing her chair back. "I don't know about those revolving planets of yours, but if you can beat that nasty bully Ben O'Brien at the Laser Lunacy, I'll buy you another ice-cream soda."

"Bully?" said Zeke. "What is that?"

"You know, beats up kids that are smaller than he is, takes their lunches and money, pushes everybody around, says nasty things," Cassie rattled off the stuff that bullies are made of until Zeke begged her to stop.

"I understand," he said as they got on the escalator to the main floor. "We have bullies on my planet, too."

The video arcade was even more crowded than the fourth floor. Zeke was a whiz at every game he played. He was especially good at Dark Invader. By the time he reached the highest plateau of the advanced level, a crowd had gathered.

"This is the most primitive space weaponry I have ever seen," Zeke said to Cassie out of the side of his mouth.

"Zeke!"

"Even for a game," Zeke added.

"Zeke!" Cassie repeated. She leaned in and whispered, "Please don't say anything stupid!"

68

It was very exciting, thought Cassie. She had never been in the center of a crowd in the arcade before. Everywhere that she and Zeke went, an ever-growing group of kids followed. As Zeke whipped through every game in the arcade, the whispered questions grew louder: Who was he? Where had he come from? Could he beat Ben O'Brien at Laser Lunacy?

But long before Ben O'Brien showed up, Marilee Tischler appeared with her usual group of followers. She pushed her way to the front of the crowd.

"Hi, Cassie."

"Hi, Marilee," said Cassie, without taking her eyes off Zeke.

"Hi, Zeke," said Marilee in the sugary voice she used to talk to boys. "Where did you disappear to today at the weather bureau?"

"Don't bother him," said Cassie. "He's concentrating."

"I'm tired of this game anyway," said Zeke. He passed the controls to a boy standing next to him. The boy attacked the game eagerly. But he had never played at the highest level before, and the game was over almost instantly. A groan rose from the crowd. The boy's face flushed red and he moved away.

"You're so *goood* at that game, Zeke." Marilee's voice oozed niceness. Cassie thought she was going to be sick. Why was Marilee so interested in

Zeke? Didn't she have enough friends already? Cassie watched the way Marilee was talking to Zeke. She had seen Lauren, a girl on her street, behaving like this last year. Lauren had told Cassie she was shopping for her first boyfriend.

Suddenly Cassie had the urge to lean over and rip off Zeke's wig. Marilee wouldn't be so interested in him then. She wouldn't want her first boyfriend to be bald.

"Hi, Cassie," said Melinda.

"Hi, Melinda." Cassie spoke to her old friend absently, her eyes on Zeke and Marilee.

"You know, I've been thinking about something," said Melinda.

"What's that?"

"How could you have a cousin? I thought both of your parents were only children."

Cassie's head swiveled, and her eyes met Melinda's.

"He's, um, a second cousin, I guess."

"How are you related to him?" Melinda persisted.

Loud voices at the entrance to the arcade were music to Cassie's ears. She'd have time to think of an answer before Melinda asked the question again.

Ben O'Brien was picking a fight with a smaller kid who was in the middle of a game of Laser Lunacy. He yelled and poked until the smaller boy moved away.

"The bully?" Zeke mouthed to Cassie. Cassie nodded her head.

Zeke stood patiently near the back of the crowd while Ben moved smoothly through the game. Fifteen minutes later, Ben was warmed up.

"Challengers?" he growled. A group of boys moved away from the front of the crowd.

"I challenge you," Zeke called out, moving forward slowly until he was standing in front of the bully. Ben looked the alien up and down.

"I don't know you," he snarled.

"Well, I know of you," said Zeke.

They moved to their positions. Zeke quickly scanned the written directions on the control panel. He was reading the last line when a roar went up from the group behind him. Ben had slipped the quarters in and started the game. He was already ahead by eight hundred points.

Zeke gripped the controls and launched into the game. He handled the controls expertly, shooting laser blasts at ever-moving targets and dodging deadly missiles fired from Ben's gun. Ben was good. He was indeed a master at blasting satellites and roving stars. But Zeke was better at attacking Ben's fuel plants, the highest-scoring move in the game.

In no time at all Zeke had shortened Ben's lead. By the beginning of the final round, they were tied. Cassie could see the sweat pouring down Ben's back. She was glad Zeke wasn't

sweating. His wig might slide off.

Zeke hit another fuel base, and his score sky-rocketed. He was winning! But at that instant, Ben swung his elbow out and knocked one of Zeke's hands off the controls. While Zeke struggled to get back into the game, Ben racked up point after point. In a matter of moments, he was winning again.

Cassie was the only one who saw what happened next. And that was only because of how carefully she was studying Zeke. She just couldn't believe that he would let Ben get away with the elbow trick. So while everyone else was talking about what Ben had done, Cassie was watching Zeke's hands.

The movement took two seconds. In a flash, Zeke removed something from the pocket of his jeans, touched Ben's hand, and resumed the game. Ben cried out, and his hand flew off the controls. By the time he got back in the game the score was tied again.

For a few moments Ben and Zeke were neck and neck, but then, with a flourish, Zeke blasted a final base and won. While the crowd roared in surprise and delight, Ben looked on in fury.

"You'll pay for this, boy," Ben threatened, poking a finger into Zeke's chest. "I don't know what you did. But you'll be sorry!"

And with that, Ben the Bully stomped out of the arcade.

CHAPTER 11

Zeke munched on a corndog as he and Cassie walked to the spaceship.

"So, do you have superpowers or not?" Cassie asked.

Zeke laughed. "I'm sorry to disappoint you, Cassie. But I have not discovered any superpowers yet."

"Oh yeah?" said Cassie. "What was that thing you did to Ben? That was great!"

Zeke reached into his pocket and pulled out a small metal object with prongs. "This is an electromagnorighter," he said. "I would never have used it if Ben had not cheated first.

"An electromagno . . . what?"

"It is a simple tool used for repairing robots. I carry it in case the ro—I mean, Spot, needs repairs. It emits a slight electric shock."

Zeke stopped walking.

"Cassie, I must admit that I am concerned about Spot. Would it be all right if we used a materializer to get back to the ship in a more efficient manner?"

"Sure!" Cassie grinned.

The two friends ducked behind a bush. A moment later they materialized aboard the ship. They searched every room, every nook and cranny. Spot was nowhere to be found.

"Where can he be?" said Zeke. He was looking more and more worried.

Cassie tried to comfort him. "He can't have gone far. Let's get our spy belts and have a look."

The two spies sprang into action. With their spy belts fastened firmly around their waists and some of Zeke's choice spy-academy gadgets stuffed in their pockets, Cassie and the spy from outer space materialized at the last place they had seen the robot—outside Hillsdale Elementary School.

The schoolyard was empty, which was just fine with Cassie and Zeke. It wasn't as if they could go around asking people if they'd seen a robot disguised as a dog.

"Look for signs of a struggle," Zeke told Cassie as they prepared to snoop around.

"Why?" asked Cassie.

"That is standard procedure in the case of all possible kidnappings," the alien replied.

"Kidnappings?" said Cassie. "What makes you think Spot was kidnapped?"

"Logic," said Zeke. "Spot was ordered to protect me."

"Yeah, well, you ordered him to go back to the ship," said Cassie.

"Exactly," said Zeke. "So if he wasn't waiting for us here and he wasn't aboard the spaceship, he was obviously kidnapped."

"Good point," said Cassie. "Ready?"

"Ready," said Zeke.

Cassie climbed the tallest tree and scanned the horizon with her binoculars while Zeke poked among the ground-level bushes. They communicated by walkie-talkie.

"Playground area clean," reported Zeke.

"Acknowledged," said Cassie. "No sign of trouble on the eastern horizon."

"Approaching the back of the school," Zeke said into his walkie-talkie.

"Western horizon clear," reported Cassie.

Slowly and very carefully, the two spies combed the entire area. But there was no sign of Spot. Half an hour later, Cassie and Zeke met at the exact place where they had last seen him.

"There's just no sign of a struggle here," said Zeke. He sounded discouraged.

Cassie bent down and looked at the ground. "Maybe there is, Zeke," she said.

Zeke crouched down beside his friend. "What makes you say that?"

"Look here," said Cassie, pointing at the dirt.

"We know Spot was right here. Yet there are no imprints of his strange metal feet. There are no footprints at all in this area. Just dirt that looks like it was brushed recently."

"You're right!" Zeke exclaimed. "But look! There *are* footprints—right here!"

Zeke pointed to an area of dirt several feet away. Cassie peered at the large footprints.

"Those are human prints," said Cassie. "Very large human prints. Sneakers, I'd say."

"Larger than the ones a child in this school would make," said Zeke.

"Absolutely," Cassie agreed.

"Cassie, I have an idea. Give me the razimizer."

"Excuse me?" said Cassie.

"The larger metal object I gave you on the ship. You put it in the left pocket of your jacket."

Cassie reached into her pocket and handed Zeke a tubular, hollow device. Zeke flipped a switch at one end of the gadget, and a low humming sound began.

"What does it do?" asked Cassie.

"It detects metal," said Zeke. "If the robot was damaged at all, there might be metal shavings around."

Zeke combed a large area surrounding the last place they had seen Spot. He found two pennies, one quarter, and a broken barrette. But not even one metal shaving.

"Perhaps we should search the inside of the

building," Zeke called to Cassie, who was bent over about three yards away.

"I don't think that will be necessary," Cassie called back. She stood up and walked toward Zeke.

"Look!" she said, holding out her arm. In her hand was a wig. "It has glue on it. It definitely came off of Spot."

"Kidnapped!" said Zeke, taking the wig from Cassie.

"Kidnapped," Cassie agreed.

Back on board the spaceship, Zeke and Cassie sipped melted Jell-O for spying strength and tried to figure out who would kidnap Spot.

"It could be almost anyone," said Cassie. "I mean, who *wouldn't* take an alien robot if they found one?"

"What if they didn't know he was from another planet?" said Zeke.

"What do you mean?"

"What if they thought he really was a dog? Do people kidnap animals on this planet?"

Cassie thought about it.

"Yes. I think they do, sometimes," she said. "Then they sell them for money."

"So maybe the robot was kidnapped by a dog-napper," Zeke said triumphantly.

"Dognapper, that's good!" Cassie said, laughing. Then she jumped up off her seat.

"That's it!" she cried.

"What's it?" Zeke exclaimed, jumping off his chair and joining her.

"When we were at the weather bureau, I saw a dogcatcher's van. I thought it was kind of strange, but I didn't make the connection. That's it! That's it!" Cassie was dancing around the room.

"What's it? What connection? Stop jumping!" said Zeke.

Cassie stopped moving around. But she was so excited, she was practically yelling at Zeke.

"I know where Spot is. That guy by the garbage cans—the one I couldn't see—he was a dogcatcher. That's what he meant when he said he caught something strange. That's why his van was there. The dogcatcher caught Spot!"

"Okay!" Zeke yelled back. "Where does the dogcatcher take the dogs?"

"The Hillsdale Pound, of course!" Cassie exclaimed. "Let's go!"

Barbed wire surrounded the Hillsdale Pound. By the shadowy light of the rising moon, two figures, clothed all in black, peered up at the spiked fence.

"Okay, Earth spy, what do we do now?" Zeke whispered into the night.

"Break in, of course," Cassie grinned.

"I am curious as to the type of metal used in this fence," said Zeke. He reached out to touch the barbed wire.

"Zeke, no!" cried Cassie. But it was too late. As Zeke's hand touched the fence, Cassie heard a sizzling sound and watched in horror as the alien lit up like a Christmas tree. He moaned softly and crumpled to the ground. Cassie raced to his side.

"Zeke! Are you all right?" Cassie knelt down and gently touched Zeke's shoulder.

"Wha . . . what happened?" asked Zeke, sitting up, the hairs from his wig standing straight up in the air.

"That's an electrified fence. I tried to warn you."

"How did you know this fence was electric?"

"I didn't. I just thought it might be, that's all. Are you okay?"

"I believe so," said Zeke, rising to his feet. Cassie stood up, too.

"That was a much larger shock than the one I delivered to Ben O'Brien in the mall," Zeke said, grinning.

"You're telling me," said Cassie. She looked at Zeke and burst out laughing.

"I wish Ben's hair had looked like yours does now after you shocked him!"

Zeke's hand flew to his hair, self-consciously.

"There are benefits to having no hair," he said.

A howl from inside the pound echoed through the night air. Cassie shivered and looked around.

"Let's rescue Spot and get out of here," she said.

"How?" asked Zeke.

In silence, they studied the fence. It surrounded the pound and was as high as a two story building.

"It really is too bad that you can't fly," Cassie said softly.

"That's it!" said Zeke.

"What's it?"

"I *can* fly, Cassie. Without this!" Zeke pulled the gravitonizer from his pocket and dropped it on the ground. In an instant, he shot up into the air.

"Kick yourself over the wire!" Cassie called up to Zeke.

Zeke kicked his feet and soared across the barbed wire and into the pound. Cassie retrieved the gravitonizer and threw it to her friend. He caught it in his left hand and gently drifted back to earth.

"What now?" Zeke asked Cassie through the fence.

"Find the door, break the lock, and get Spot, of course!" said Cassie. "I assume you have some great spy device that breaks locks."

"Of course," said Zeke. "Only, it melts them."

Another howl rose from inside the pound. Cassie shivered.

"Hurry up, Zeke. Don't leave me out here all night."

Zeke found the door. Cassie squinted in the dark and tried to see what he was doing. A moment later, the Triminican disappeared into the building.

Cassie waited for what seemed an eternity. When Zeke finally reappeared, he was alone.

"What happened?" asked Cassie. "Where's Spot?"

"I don't know," said Zeke. "I saw many strange animals in there. They keep them in cages. But the robot was not inside any of them."

Cassie sighed. "I'm sorry, Zeke. I was sure Spot was in there."

"It was a good idea, Cassie. It is not your fault that we did not locate the robot here."

Zeke looked so sad that Cassie was afraid he might cry. She wondered if Triminicans had tear ducts.

"We'll find him, Zeke."

Zeke nodded and sighed, a habit he was picking up from Cassie.

"Zeke, I really have to get home now. I've already missed dinner, and my parents are going to be worried. Can we search for Spot again tomorrow?"

"Of course," said Zeke. With her help he crossed over the fence. Then he handed her a materializer disk. He had already set the coordinates for her house.

"Good night, Zeke," said Cassie.

"Good night, Cassie."

Cassie stepped back from the fence and threw the golden disk. As the rings of sparkling light surrounded her, Cassie glanced at Zeke once more. He was looking sadly at the pound.

After a ten-minute lecture on the importance of coming home on time, Cassie's mother handed her a stack of messages. Marilee Tischler had called. So had Melinda, and Ben O'Brien. Mrs. Williams told Cassie how thrilled she was that

Cassie was making new friends. If only she knew, thought Cassie, my best friend is an alien.

Cassie returned all the calls. Marilee wanted to talk to Zeke. Cassie hung up on that problem, deciding to worry about it later. At the moment, it wasn't as important as finding Spot.

Then Cassie called Melinda. It was the first time she'd dialed her old friend's number in weeks.

"Don't you think it's funny the way Marilee is acting around Zeke?" asked Melinda, after they'd said their hellos.

"She acts that way around a lot of boys," said Cassie.

"That's what I mean," giggled Melinda. "It's like she thinks she's in high school or something."

Cassie took a deep breath.

"Do you like boys?" she asked.

"Yeah, sure," said Melinda. "I mean. Well—no. Not the way Marilee does. Do you?"

"No," said Cassie.

"Zeke *is* kind of cute," said Melinda.

"I know," said Cassie.

"Cassie! He's your cousin!"

Cassie felt trapped.

"He is your cousin, isn't he?" asked Melinda.

"I've got to go, Melinda. My mother's calling me. See you in school tomorrow. Bye."

Cassie hung up the phone and breathed a

shaky sigh of relief. Life was getting very complicated. First the man at the weather bureau, now Ben O'Brien, Marilee, and Melinda. Cassie was beginning to wonder how long she could keep Zeke's identity a secret. And where in the world was Spot?

Spot was on TV. Or rather, they were talking about him on TV. When Cassie went into the family room to kiss her father good night, a large, burly man wearing a baseball cap that said Dogcatcher was being interviewed by a reporter.

"I don't know what it was," grumbled the man. Cassie immediately recognized his voice. It was the man from outside the weather bureau.

"It was a dog, sort of. But it was the weirdest dog I've ever seen."

"And after catching this animal, you put him in the back of your truck with the other dogs?" asked the reporter.

"Yeah," grunted the dogcatcher. "And then I took him to the pound."

"And then what happened?" The reporter urged the man to continue.

"Well." The man took off his cap and scratched his head. "I'm not sure. He escaped."

"How?" asked the reporter.

"I don't know. One minute he was in his cage, and the next minute he wasn't. The lock was broken. I couldn't find him anywhere."

The reporter faced the camera.

"So there you have it. A mysterious-looking dog who opens locks and disappears into the night. But *was* it a dog? And where is it now? This reporter would like to know."

Mr. Williams laughed and turned off the TV. When he looked at his daughter, she was frozen in place, her mouth hanging open.

"Don't believe everything you see on TV, honey," said Mr. Williams, as he kissed Cassie on the cheek. "Isn't it time for bed?"

"What? Uh, yeah," said Cassie. "Night, Dad."

In a daze, Cassie turned and wandered into the hallway. She climbed the stairs to her room and got ready for bed. But she knew she wasn't going to get any sleep at all. Spot was lost somewhere in Hillsdale, and now there were people looking for him.

Early the next morning, Cassie pounded on the golden door. The staircase descended, and she clambered on board.

"Zeke! Zeke!" she called, waving a newspaper in the air.

"I'm in here." Cassie followed the sound of Zeke's voice and found him in the kitchen cooking what smelled like French toast.

"Good morning," said Zeke. "Would you care for a meal before school?"

"Zeke, look!" Cassie shoved the paper in front of Zeke's face just as he was flipping a piece of egg-drenched bread into a sizzling pan. Both the spatula and the bread landed on the floor as Zeke grabbed at the paper.

"Read it out loud," said Cassie, as she cleaned up the mess.

Zeke read the headline: "Unidentified Creature Scares Animals in Zoo!" He continued, "An unidentified creature was found wandering the town of Hillsdale last night. Zoo officials were contacted, and the creature was housed in a special cage in the Hillsdale Zoo overnight. When zookeepers gathered to inspect the creature early this morning, it was gone."

"All right, Spot!" said Cassie, standing up and rinsing out her sponge.

Zeke read on. "Upon further examination, many of the animals in the zoo were behaving as if they had received a terrible fright. Especially the lions, who cowered in a corner of their cage. The creature, who vaguely resembles a dog, is believed to be the same animal that escaped from the pound yesterday. Officials are fairly certain the creature is still somewhere inside the zoo, possibly hiding, and probably scared. If you see this animal, do not attempt to touch it. Contact zoo officials immediately."

Zeke put his head in his hands and groaned. "Mirac will be furious," he said.

"Mirac will never know," said Cassie. "They don't get this newspaper in Hawaii."

"Really?" Zeke brightened.

"Really," said Cassie. "And maybe Spot will show up here today."

"What is this 'zoo'?" asked Zeke.

"It's where we keep all the animals so we can see what they look like," said Cassie.

"You take them out of their natural habitat and cage them?" asked Zeke. "Like at that 'pound' we saw yesterday?"

"You sound like my mother!" snapped Cassie.

"You know, Cassie, we don't have any animals on Triminica," said Zeke. "Long ago, all the animals in our galaxy were transported to another planet."

"And they live in absolute harmony, right?" said Cassie in her most sarcastic voice.

"They live as they live," said Zeke. "I have never been there."

Cassie studied Zeke for a moment. She knew the look on his face. The same look had been on her face for almost an entire month at Camp Sunny Lake last year. The spy from outer space was homesick.

"We have lots of time before school," said Cassie. "Let's walk today. I can show you more of Hillsdale that way. And maybe later today we can go to the planetarium and find your planet among the stars."

"That would be nice," said Zeke. "Perhaps another day. Right now, I think I'd like to go to the zoo."

"But what about school?" asked Cassie. "I've never cut classes before."

"You do not have to accompany me," said Zeke.

Cassie tried to figure out which would be worse—missing school or reading in tomorrow's paper that Zeke was another animal caught and caged in the zoo. A shiver ran down her spine as she thought about the conversation she had overheard at the weather bureau. She decided a day away from school was exactly what she needed.

The zoo was crawling with people. There were reporters and police officers and plenty of parents with their kids. Everyone had come to catch a glimpse of Spot.

Zeke and Cassie got off the bus and stood in the long ticket line. They had decided not to use the materializers. Spot was drawing enough attention to "unidentified creatures." They wanted to appear as normal as possible.

Once inside, the spies pushed their way to the front of the throng at the lion's cage.

"I heard it was a giant sheepdog—over ten feet tall," said a woman near Cassie.

"No, Ma!" whined a child. "It was a ten-foot-tall *giant* who *looked* like a sheepdog."

"Actually, I heard it was a robot dog," said a man. "Probably a marketing trick from a toy company."

"Do you see anything?" Cassie whispered to Zeke.

"What am I looking for?" Zeke whispered back.

"Spot, of course. Or some sign of him."

"Robots do not leave signs."

"Well, maybe he's waiting somewhere to be rescued, and he left a clue."

Zeke peered into the cage at a lion lounging on a rock.

"That is a lion?" he said, and laughed.

"I wouldn't laugh at a lion if I were you," said Cassie. "To him, you look like an afternoon snack."

"He looks very much like a mecurtian," said Zeke.

"An animal that used to be on your planet?" asked Cassie.

"Mecurtians are humanoids," said Zeke. "They are much larger than us and have great manes. Just like the lion here."

"I guess you wouldn't go to their planet for vacation," Cassie said, and grinned.

"The mecurtians are gentle," said Zeke. "And they have knowledge and skills far beyond ours."

Cassie and Zeke moved from exhibit to exhibit, searching everywhere for Spot. The day passed quickly—too quickly. Zeke was having a wonderful time looking at all the Earth animals, but the sky was growing dark. And they still hadn't seen any sign of the robot.

A voice over a loudspeaker announced that the park was closing in twenty minutes.

"Maybe he found his way back to the ship," said Cassie hopefully.

"Maybe," said Zeke doubtfully. "If not, I will have to return here tomorrow."

"Sure, Zeke," said Cassie softly. "I'll come with you."

On the way to the exit, they passed the monkey house. Cassie grabbed Zeke's arm.

"Let's go in here for a minute," she said. "It's my favorite part of the zoo." Zeke let Cassie lead him into the dimly lit building.

"Can't you see how much they look like us?" Cassie said to Zeke as they watched a family of apes swing from tree to tree.

"Only as much as a creptori looks like a sagebool," said Zeke.

"You know, Zeke," said Cassie, "sometimes talking to you is like talking to someone from another planet."

Zeke burst out laughing. Cassie laughed, too. In fact, she laughed so hard that when she looked into the gorilla cage she could barely choke out the words, "Look. Spot!"

Zeke lunged for the place where Cassie was pointing, but he was blocked by a thick plate-glass window.

"Zeke, calm down," whispered Cassie. "There are people here. Just look at him for now."

Spot was hanging from a tree in the back of the gorilla cage. He was half hidden by a female gorilla who seemed to have taken a liking to him.

"What should we do?" asked Zeke, his voice rising.

"Nothing, right now," said Cassie. "And let's move away from the cage. Maybe no one else will notice him."

Outside the monkey house, Cassie and Zeke sat on a bench and planned. By the time the voice on the loudspeaker announced the closing of the zoo, the spies were ready. Mixing in with a group of parents and small children, they headed for the exit. When they reached the tropical bird house to the right of the entrance gate, they dived behind the building to hide.

When the last of the guests had exited, an eerie silence settled over the zoo. The only sound was the occasional cry of a bird.

Moving swiftly and close to the ground, the spies reached a small hill across from the monkey house. Cassie pulled out her binoculars and focused them on the building's entrance. A zoo employee swept dirt from the path in front. Then he fastened a huge, sturdy padlock on the heavy metal door.

"How are we going to break the lock?" Cassie whispered.

Zeke's eyes twinkled in the dark.

"Zorcanian 6, of course," he whispered back.

"Of course," said Cassie. "Uh—what's zorcanian 6?"

"It is a metal dissolver," said Zeke. "I used it to break the lock at the pound." He reached into his jacket pocket and pulled out what looked like a small ray gun.

"Do you always carry metal dissolvers with you?" asked Cassie.

"On an unfamiliar planet, spies of the Interstellar Spy Academy carry many supplies," said Zeke. He reached into another pocket and pulled out a handful of strange-looking objects.

Cassie looked at Zeke's hand and laughed. His fingernails had grown at least an inch since he had cut them, and they were starting to curl at the ends.

"You're going to have to clip those again," she said, touching one of Zeke's nails.

"But they are so practical," said Zeke, using two fingernails to pluck a small hollow tube of some sort of plastic out of his hand. He held it up for Cassie to see.

"This is a weapon used for stunning the enemy," Zeke explained.

"It looks like a peashooter," said Cassie.

The spies were suddenly plunged into darkness as someone turned off all the lights in the zoo.

"Let's go!" said Zeke.

"Just a minute," said Cassie. "Exactly how are we going to break into the gorilla cage?" she asked.

"I have been thinking about that," said Zeke. "I am fairly certain that the robot can do it himself. I just have to tell him how."

"If he could escape, why hasn't he already?" asked Cassie.

"He is probably afraid he will get caught again."

Cassie giggled. "He did look pretty cozy in there."

"That is not funny, Cassie."

"I know," said Cassie. "I just hope we get him out before dinner. My mother will kill me if I'm late again."

Zeke was silent. Cassie dropped her eyes from the binoculars and looked at her friend.

"Zeke?"

"I was just thinking about my mother. I wonder where she is."

"You know where she is. She's in Hawaii. She's perfectly safe, and she and your father will be home soon."

"Thanks, Cassie."

"Anytime," said Cassie. She hoped she was right.

"Cassie, look!"

Cassie's eyes darted to the entrance of the monkey house. The two men had left. She scanned the rest of the grounds once with her naked eyes, then used the binoculars to search again.

There was no one. They were alone.

The spies sprang into action. They raced down the hill to the monkey house. Cassie stared at the padlock.

"Let's have some of that Triminican magic," she said.

Zeke aimed the ray gun carefully at the lock. He pressed the trigger. A spray of amber liquid coated the lock. A minute later, the lock melted into a puddle.

"Amazing!" Cassie whispered.

Zeke smiled, obviously pleased with himself.

The two friends slipped in through the door and headed straight for the gorilla cage. Spot was still hanging from the branch.

"Spot!" Zeke called into the cage.

"It's very thick glass," said Cassie. "He won't be able to hear you."

"Spot has incredible hearing," said Zeke. He banged on the window and called Spot's name again.

The robot heard the banging and moved his body so he could see Zeke and Cassie. The female gorilla woke from a nap. The robot dropped from the tree and made his way to the front of the cage. The female followed.

"Spot has a girlfriend," giggled Cassie.

"This is not funny, Cassie," said Zeke. "Something is wrong with the robot. He looks almost upset. I think these creatures have had an effect on him."

"I thought he didn't really have emotions," said Cassie.

"That is not exactly true," Zeke explained. "He does not have emotions like ours. But he does have feelings—sort of."

The female gorilla threw her arms around Spot. The robot went into a frenzy. He struggled in the embrace, turning his body around and around, jabbering in a language Cassie had never heard before.

"What's he doing?" she asked.

"He is trying to communicate with the creature," said Zeke.

Cassie watched as the gorilla got a firm grip around Spot and lifted him into the air.

Spot spun around and around but could not get loose from the embrace. Strange beeps and whirs were coming from him, and his arms and legs jerked back and forth.

"Uh-oh," said Zeke. "He's really in a bad way."

"A bad way?" said Cassie, her voice rising. "What does that mean? What is he going to do?"

"I don't know," said Zeke. "I've never seen him like this."

Spot was all motion and noise. But the gorilla hung tightly to his metal body.

"Zeke, do something!" cried Cassie.

Spot had picked up momentum. He spun so quickly in the gorilla's arms that Cassie was getting dizzy watching. Suddenly tiny sparks flew from the robot's body. The gorilla let out a horrible wail and threw the robot right through the plate-glass window! Cassie and Zeke screamed and ducked for cover.

After a moment, Cassie looked up. She gasped. The entire window of the gorilla cage had been shattered. Two of the beasts had already escaped and were heading for the entrance to the monkey house. More were following in their path.

"Zeke?" Cassie called.

"Over here," said Zeke. "I've got Spot. Let's go!"

Cassie made her way to the corner of the room where Zeke cradled a sizzling Spot in his arms. Footsteps and human voices could be heard outside the building.

"Throw the disk!" said Cassie.

Zeke punched numbers quickly and threw the disk into the air. Just before the circling lights transported them to the ship, half a dozen armed men burst in through the doors.

In the darkness outside the monkey house, Grant Trexler clutched a copy of the *Hillsdale News* in his hand and grinned.

CHAPTER

15

Cassie started talking the minute they touched down inside the spaceship.

"This is awful! I can just see the papers tomorrow morning. There will be gorillas everywhere. Everyone in town is going to be searching for Spot! What if they track him here? What if they saw us? What if that scientist reads about him? What are we going to do?"

"Cassie, calm down!" said Zeke.

Cassie stopped talking and pacing long enough to glance over at her friend. Zeke was crouched over Spot, checking him carefully for damage.

Spot was beaten up pretty badly. His side was dented, and one of his arms had been ripped off. A thin, steady stream of smoke rose from one of his eye sockets.

"Oh, Spot," said Cassie. She knelt down beside Zeke and gazed at the broken robot.

"Can you fix him?" she asked.

Zeke shook his head. "I don't think so." He sighed. "I've really made a mess of things."

"It isn't your fault, Zeke," said Cassie. She glanced at her watch and gasped. "Oh no! I completely forgot about dinner."

A sound like a firecracker echoed through the ship.

"What was that?" asked Cassie.

"That was the robot, I am afraid," said Zeke. "Cassie, I think perhaps you should return home. I will have to stay up all night trying to fix him."

"But what about school tomorrow?"

"The trouble you will be in when you return home at this late hour is nothing compared to what will happen to me when Mirac returns and sees the robot."

Cassie peered down at Spot. He looked dead. Then she looked at Zeke. He looked as though he had lost his best friend. She didn't think that fear of Mirac was the real reason Zeke would stay up all night fixing Spot. The robot was Zeke's friend.

"Try to show up for school, okay?" said Cassie.

But Zeke was already taking Spot apart, examining each piece carefully before he set it aside.

"You know where the disks are," he said without looking up. "Don't take more than you need."

The first sound Cassie heard when she materialized was a scream. She looked up from her rather awkward position on the desk in her bedroom—the result of a slight mistake in setting the coordinates—and there was her brother, pointing at her and howling.

"Simon! What are you doing in my room?"

"Where did you come from, Cass?"

"Why did you scream?"

"How did you get on the desk?"

Back and forth they shouted frenzied questions at each other. Finally, Cassie scrambled down from the desk and locked the door to her room. She sat on the bed and motioned for Simon to do the same. He sat down, but on the other side of the bed, facing her, studying her.

"Okay, Simon," Cassie said slowly. "I'll ask a question, and you answer it. And then you ask a question, and I'll answer it. Okay?"

Simon shrugged.

"I'll go first," said Cassie. "What were you doing in my room?"

"Where did you come from?"

Cassie sighed. This wasn't working, and she really didn't have the time or patience to play twenty questions. She leaned over and grabbed her brother by the shoulders.

"Simon, where are Mom and Dad?"

"Out looking for you."

"What?"

"The monkeys escaped from the zoo, Cass,"

said Simon. He wriggled to get out of her grasp, but Cassie kept her hands clamped down on his shoulders.

"How do you know that, Simon?"

"The monkeys escaped from the zoo and carried people away. How'd you land on the desk?"

"I, uh, meant to land on the floor," Cassie answered honestly. She let go of Simon's shoulders and jumped up from the bed. She started pacing and biting her fingernails. There were too many things to think about all at once. Why were her parents out looking for her? Just how many gorillas had escaped from the zoo? Who had they carried off? Had anyone seen Zeke or Spot in the monkey house? Had anyone seen her?

"Cass?" Her little brother's voice interrupted her thinking.

"What is it, Simon?"

"Can we watch the monkeys on TV?"

Cassie grinned at her brother. He really was smart.

"That's a great idea!"

She grabbed Simon's hand and yanked him off the bed and down the stairs to the family room. Simon laughed the whole way. Cassie wasn't sure if it was because his feet barely touched the ground or the fact that they weren't supposed to watch television on a school night.

Every channel carried the story. Gorillas broke the plate-glass window in the monkey house. No one knows how or why it happened. Could there be a link to the mysterious creature captured yesterday? More news at eleven . . .

Just then the doorbell rang. It was her former friend, Melinda, and Marilee Tischler.

"What are you doing here?" asked Cassie.

"I've come to see Zeke," said Marilee in her soppiest voice.

"Oh, really?"

"Who's Zeke?" Simon's voice chirped behind her.

Cassie slammed the door in Marilee's face and turned to Simon.

"I will buy you three chocolate bars tomorrow if you pretend that you were kidding and that Zeke is your cousin who is staying with us. Okay?"

Simon shrugged his shoulders.

"Sorry about that." Cassie smiled as she opened the door again. "It must have slipped."

There was no way Marilee believed the door had slipped, but at least she wasn't rude enough to deny it. And even though Melinda wasn't saying much of anything, Cassie noticed that she was doing a lot of squirming. Good.

Marilee bent down and talked in a baby voice to Simon. "Did you say, 'Who's Zeke?'"

Simon shrugged.

"Do you know who Zeke is?" Marilee's voice was getting gooier and gooier. Cassie breathed a sigh of relief. Simon absolutely hated it when anyone talked to him that way. If his love for his sister—and the promise of candy bars—hadn't been enough, Marilee's voice would see to it that Simon lied.

"I know," said Simon.

"Who is he?" demanded Marilee.

"He's my cousin the alien who's come to stay with us!" Simon announced proudly.

Cassie was stunned. Where had Simon come up with the bit about the alien? Did he know more than he let on? Or was he just being his usual over imaginative self?

But when Melinda and Marilee laughed and said how cute Simon was, Cassie realized his answer was the best thing that could have happened.

"Well?" said Marilee cheerily. "Is Zeke here or not?

"He's busy," said Cassie. "What do you want?"

"Not that it's any of your business," snapped Marilee. "But there's a science competition coming up, and you have to enter in a boy-girl team."

"So?"

"So, I wanted to ask Zeke to be my partner."

"At eight o'clock at night? With all the monkeys loose from the zoo? You just *had* to come over to ask a boy you don't even know to be your partner for a stupid science competition?"

"Actually," Melinda said softly, "we're just coming back from the zoo. Everyone was there, Cassie. You should have been there, too."

"Why?" snapped Cassie. "To see men shooting poor monkeys and putting them back in cages?"

"They use tranquilizer guns!" Marilee said snottily. "And all it does is make the dumb animals sleep."

All Cassie could think of to say was that Marilee was a dumb animal. But it was the kind of comment that she would be sorry for later on. So she ignored Marilee and talked directly to Melinda.

"Simon says that the gorillas were carrying people off. Is that true?"

"I'm not sure," said Melinda. "There *was* a rumor that one of the really big ones had carried off some kid. So every parent whose kid didn't happen to be home started freaking out and driving around looking for them."

"So, can I see Zeke or not?" demanded Marilee.

Cassie smiled her best sickly-sweet smile. "The truth is, Marilee, he's already got a partner for the science competition. Me."

"But he's your cousin!" said Marilee.

"So?" said Cassie. "There's no law against it, is there? It's not like we're getting married or anything."

Cassie's parents chose that particular moment to drive up to the house. They had returned to pick up Simon and continue searching for Cassie.

But here she was safe and sound. Somehow everyone managed to exchange hellos and hugs without the subject of Zeke coming up again. Melinda and Marilee left, and the Williams family went inside to discover a burned meatloaf and charred potatoes for dinner.

The whole family piled back into the car and headed for their favorite restaurant on the other side of town. As they pulled out of the driveway, Cassie was the only one who saw Ben O'Brien banging on the front door.

Mr. Williams sped down a highway that ran along the empty field where Cassie had first seen the spaceship. Cassie stared out the window, and her thoughts turned to Zeke and Spot. She hoped the repairs were going well.

Cassie's mind was so far away that she didn't notice the gorilla loping beside the car.

CHAPTER

16

Zeke wasn't in school the next day. Neither were a lot of kids. According to all reports, one gorilla still ran loose in Hillsdale, and many parents refused to allow their children to go to school until it was caught. Mrs. Williams insisted on driving Cassie to school, though she said that she doubted an ape would want to attend Hillsdale Elementary any more than Cassie did.

While Cassie sat in class, Grant Trexler waited outside the school. He still clutched a copy of the *Hillsdale News* in one hand and a rough sketch he had drawn of Cassie in the other.

Grant saw Cassie the moment she left the school building. But the young spy was so eager to find out if Zeke had fixed Spot that she didn't notice the man following her.

When Cassie reached the open field near where the ship was hidden, she broke into a run. Several hundred yards away from the edge of the forest she had to stop and rest. But as she paused to catch her breath, she heard a sound behind her. Her heart leapt into her throat and she turned.

A man was racing across the field, gaining in the distance. Cassie squinted into the sun and saw a flash of light leap off the man's face. She had seen the sun dance off those eyeglasses before, and the lump grew in her throat as she realized who was following her. She jumped to her feet and started running again. But as she reached the first few trees of the forest, Cassie suddenly realized that she was leading Grant right to the aliens.

Quickly Cassie darted out into the open field again. She turned as she ran to see if Grant was still behind her. But he had paused by the trees and was peering among them, searching. He stepped farther, until he was almost hidden. Cassie stopped running and watched, holding her breath. What would she do if he found the ship? How could she get him to follow her again? Cassie's mind was racing, and her hands were sweating. She started slowly toward the forest.

Suddenly there was a scream. And a growl. And a rustling of trees and a roar. A huge gorilla burst out of the brush, holding Grant Trexler in her arms. Cassie watched, her mouth open and her eyes wide, as the two disappeared across the field.

Cassie dashed into the trees. When she reached the ship, she called up to Zeke.

"Cassie!" cried Zeke as he lowered the stairs. "What's going on out there? I heard a scream."

"I was being followed," Cassie said, gasping for air.

"By whom?" asked Zeke.

"The guy from the other day at the weather bureau." Cassie caught her breath and suddenly grinned. "But don't worry, an ape got him."

"Are you serious?" asked Zeke, peering out of the ship's window.

Cassie nodded. "Yep. He's gone for now. How's Spot?"

"Come aboard and see for yourself."

Cassie took the steps two at a time. Spot was waiting for her just inside the ship.

"SPOT!" Cassie called out. She leapt across the room and threw her arms around the metal body.

"Cassie, don't hug him!" Zeke said, alarmed. "Remember the zoo!"

"I do not mind this," the metallic voice droned. "This Earth creature has neither the strength nor the smell of the other."

Cassie laughed and dropped her arms.

"I thought you didn't have a good sense of smell," she said to Spot. Spot ignored her and moved away.

"Zeke, how did you do it?" Cassie asked.

"He had some help," said a voice from behind Cassie. She whirled around and found herself facing Mirac.

"You're back!"

"It is good to see you, too, Cassie," said Mirac.

Inora entered the room behind her husband. She and Cassie hugged.

"How are you, Cassie? You have been a friend to my family. It is good to see you."

"How'd you fix Spot?" Cassie asked.

"Spot?"

Zeke laughed. "It's a long story." He turned to Cassie. "Mirac can fix anything," he said proudly.

"How was your trip to Hawaii?" Cassie asked.

"Most useful and informative," said Mirac. "Our trip into the volcano was a unique experience."

"And we did manage to locate the raw materials we need," said Inora.

"Then the ship is repaired?" Zeke asked eagerly.

"Not yet," responded Mirac. "There is much work to be done, and I have spent the past several hours repairing the robot. His assistance will be necessary."

"Mirac estimates our return to Triminica the day after tomorrow," said Inora.

Zeke whipped off his wig and threw it in the air with a yelp of glee.

But as he caught it, his eyes fell upon Cassie, and the grin faded from his face. The two spies stood looking at each other, saying nothing. It was somehow not a time for words.

"It's okay, Zeke," Cassie finally said. "I've had friends move before."

"Perhaps we can spend tomorrow at your planet museum," said Zeke. He turned to Inora.

"Would that be okay?"

"Of course," said Inora, smiling. "Spend your last day on Earth with your friend."

Cassie wanted to stay on the ship all day and listen to Hawaiian tales and stories of outer space. But she had to return home. Besides, she told herself as she accepted a materializer disk from Zeke, tomorrow was Saturday. She could spend the entire day with her friend before he returned home and left her on Earth, spying all alone.

CHAPTER

17

The night sky spilled out around Cassie, filling her with comfort and awe. She snuggled down into her seat and propped her head on the back of the chair. When she looked to her left, Zeke had done the same.

"Born in the darkness of interstellar space some 4.6 billion years ago, our solar system emerged from a contracting molecular cloud of dust and gas," said a deep, musical voice, filling the auditorium.

Cassie fell into the voice, the stars, and the darkness. She didn't understand everything that was said, but she understood the vastness of the universe. She knew she had to accept the long, long distance between her galaxy and the one that Zeke and his family would travel back to tomorrow. Zeke's galaxy was beyond the sun, beyond Jupiter and Saturn and Neptune. It was farther than the farthest star that astronomers on Earth had seen through their telescopes. It was definitely farther away than any of her friends had moved before.

When the show ended and the lights of the auditorium blocked out the twinkling stars, Cassie and Zeke sat in silence. As the humans around them fumbled for their purses and schoolbags, Cassie turned to Zeke.

"Do you have a lot of friends on your planet?" she asked.

"I have friends," said Zeke.

"Do they like to spy? I mean, even the ones that aren't in the spy academy?"

"Yes," said Zeke. "And sometimes I am invited to play spy games with them, and sometimes I am not."

"I would always invite you," said Cassie.

"And I would always accept," said Zeke.

"Even if you thought you were too grown up to spy?" asked Cassie.

"I will always want to be a spy," said Zeke.

They rose from their seats and left the auditorium. They wandered through all the rooms of the planetarium, gazing at this planet and that star. They stepped on giant scales and weighed themselves on Mercury and Mars. They studied the star charts of every galaxy they could find. But Zeke could not locate Triminica anywhere.

The day went quickly, too quickly, for the spies from different galaxies. At the end of the day, Zeke said he wanted to ride the bus one last time, and Cassie wanted to travel by disk one last time. So they rode halfway by bus, and halfway by disk, and arrived at the spaceship just as Mirac was finishing the repairs.

"We leave at dawn," Inora told Cassie. "Would you care to eat with us?"

"I would love to. But I have to get home," said Cassie sadly. "I promised my mother I would baby-sit for my brother tonight."

"It is good to keep promises," said Inora.

"Good-bye, Cassie," said Mirac. "Thank you for everything."

"Thank *you*," said Cassie. "This is the most fun I've ever had." She bent down and said good-bye to the robot.

"Sorry about turning you into a dog, Spot," said Cassie.

"Woof," said the robot. "And arf."

Outside the ship, Zeke gave Cassie a materializer disk to return home and his wig to remember him by. Cassie gave Zeke the present she had been carrying around in her book bag all day. It was the other walkie-talkie from her spy kit.

"So we can talk to each other. Even if there will never be an answer."

"I will miss you," said Zeke.

Cassie looked at the bald alien standing before her.

"I will miss you, too," she said, choking back tears. They hugged and Zeke threw the disk. The

119

now familiar glow of twinkling lights surrounded Cassie, as she waved to Zeke one last time.

At dinner that night, all anyone in Cassie's family could talk about was the capture of the last gorilla. Zoo officials had found her about five miles outside of town, carrying a man in her arms.

"Who was the man?" asked Cassie, as casually as she could.

"That's the really strange thing," said Mr. Williams, reaching for another roll. "They wanted to take him to the hospital to be checked out, but he refused. He wouldn't give them his name or anything."

"So he's free?" asked Cassie.

"Free?" said Mr. Williams. "He's not at the zoo or the hospital, so I suppose you could say he's free. But it's not like he's a criminal."

Isn't it? thought Cassie. She was suddenly glad Zeke was returning to his planet. Grant Trexler might not exactly be a criminal, but he was certainly a dangerous man.

Cassie set her clock for precisely five minutes before sunrise. But for the first time in her life, she woke up before the alarm went off. By the time the first ray of daylight broke through the sky, Cassie was positioned with her periscope.

"Good-bye," she whispered, as she watched

the golden ship rise into the air. "Good-bye, Zeke. Good-bye, Spot."

The ship flew higher and higher and then spiraled out of Cassie's view. She continued to look, watching the stars fade as the sun lit up the sky. Only one of them seemed to gleam brighter than the rest, refusing to be outshone.

As Cassie stared at the star and wondered which one it was, it seemed to grow brighter. She blinked her eyes and looked again. In a burst of golden light, the star plummeted to earth. As it came closer and closer, Cassie realized what it was. The Triminicans were returning!

Cassie raced down the stairs and out the front door of her house. Halfway across the field, she realized she was still in her pajamas. She didn't care. By the time she reached the clearing, the ship had landed. Cassie banged on the door.

In a thicket of trees, a few feet from the ship, Grant Trexler watched. And waited.

About the Author

Debra Hess has done a fair amount of spying in her life, and is pretty sure that a few of her friends are from outer space. The author of several popular books for young readers, she lives in Brooklyn, New York, with her husband, a lot of fish, and two newts.